SING

If the body is an orchestra . . .

singing tunes the instruments.

HUM

Humming has been used since ancient times

to harmonize body, mind and spirit.

BUMBLEBEE

When lost in the grass and clover, help

Sing and Hum Bumblebee find eight hidden friends.

The cricket conducts the orchestra of seven sounds

for seven chakras.

Lum the frog. . .Vum the cat. . .Rum the dog. . .Yum the cow. . .

Hum the bee. . .Aum the coyote. . .Om the owl.

Don't forget the little rabbit with the BIG EARS that hear

the inner voice!

Sing and Hum Bumblebee

www.ivyhousebooks.com

PUBLISHED BY IVY HOUSE PUBLISHING GROUP
5122 Bur Oak Circle, Raleigh, NC 27612
United States of America
919-782-0281
www.ivyhousebooks.com

ISBN: 1-57197-428-8
Library of Congress Control Number: 2004105139

Printed in China

Dedicated to the Music
That's
In you
&
Is you

Thanks to . . .
Pat for her inspiration
Scotty for bringing us together
The Creator for the Fundamental Tone

I'm a Big, Big Bumblebee.

Everybody laughs at me.

My head is bigger than most, you see.

My wings are like a tiny flea.

My feet are big,

my legs too long.

So queen bee taught me a song.

"Sing and hum, Bumblebee,
Find your inner harmony,
Bumblebees sing and hum,
Hum, hum, hum, hum.
When you hum, Bumblebee,
You can overcome anything."

When it's hard to move

around the hive,

My buddy bees push me from behind.

Sometimes they are so hard to please.

"Sing and hum, Bumblebee.
Find your inner harmony.
Bumblebees sing and hum.
Hum. . .hum. . . .hum. . .hum.
When you hum, Bumblebee,
You can overcome anything."

But, I can hum when I am teased.

It was hard at first

Learning to fly—

Wanting to feel free in the sky.

Tangled in flowers,

I fell to the ground.

Then I heard in me

that soothing sound:

"Sing and hum, Bumblebee.

Find your inner harmony.

Bumblebees
sing and hum—

Hum. . .hum. . .hum. . .hum.

When you hum Bumblebee,

You can overcome anything."

In grass and clover,

I'm free and merry,

But it can also be

VERY SCARY.

I'm a BIG, BIG

BUMBLEBEE.

But there are things

BIGGER

THAN

ME!

I'm flying home

very soon.

Queen Bee says,

"Sing your tune."

"Sing and hum, Bumblebee,
Find your inner harmony.
Bumblebees sing and hum~
Hum. . .hum. . .hum. . .hum.
When you hum, Bumblebee,
You can overcome ANYTHING."

Sing and Hum Bumblebee

Variations on a Theme: W. A. Mozart (1756-1791)

"Twinkle, Twinkle"

Sing and hum Bum - ble bee

Find your in - ner harm - mo - ny.

Bum - ble bees sing and hum

Hum hum hum hum

When you hum Bum - ble bee

You can o - ver come a - ny thing.

To order soundtrack, book and more visit www.singandhum.com

INSPIRATION

Where there is sound there is form, sacred geometry
Where there is sound there is music, healing harmonics
Where there is sound there is voice, toning and chanting

—Wassily Kandinsky

Many say that life entered the human body by the help of music, but the truth is that life itself is music.

—Inayat Khan

Singing is a gymnasium for a child's body and soul. Singing works deeply into our children's physiology: deepening breath and heart rate, altering brain wave patterns and strengthening the immune system. It also releases endorphins, the body's pleasure hormones into the brain and body.

—Mary Thienes

Sound is a nutrient. We can either charge or discharge the nervous system by the sounds we make through both air and bone conduction.

—Alfred Tomats

Webster's defines healing as "to make sound." It might be more accurate to say "to become sound."

—John Beaulieu

CREATOR & WRITER

Mari

Mari E. Howerton, CCMSHP, has a BA in Elementary Education and has worked in early childhood for almost 30 years. She has served as Director of an Early Childhood Center, developed kindergarten curriculum and worked with special needs children. While enlisted in the Peace Corps, Mari supervised classrooms and held training for pre-school teachers for the Ministry of Education in Belize, Central America. The teachers made puppets and performed puppet shows for more than 2,000 children and teachers. For two consecutive years, the shows were broadcast to the entire country via radio, and a videotape of the performances is housed in each of the five district libraries in Belize.

Mari is a certified Cross Cultural Music and Sound for Health Practitioner from the Open Ear Center on Brain Bridge Island, Washington. This training in music is what inspired Mari to create *Sing and Hum Bumblebee*. Mari is now combining the healing power of music and sound and her love of all special children, young and old, by writing books for children. Mari lives in Raleigh, North Carolina. She is the mother of three and the grandmother of four.

Illustrator & Writer

Maya

Karen Sorensen, "Maya," is a Certified BodyTalk Practitioner, or CBP. She works with the bodymind's energic system in restoring communication as the underlying foundation of physical and emotional health.

She has a BA in Psychology and Child Development, which led to experience working with young children and a deep foundational understanding of the necessity for pathways to guide children positively. This was supportive in raising her four children.

Along with co-writing, she illustrated *Sing and Hum Bumblebee*. Her impressionist paintings study the world beyond form, revealing hidden images within nature to facilitate the awakening of illusion, or "Maya."

Karen is a singer and a songwriter and has composed and staged children's musicals. Her work with music and healing led to the investigation of frequencies in music and how certain tones harmonize body, mind and spirit, orchestrating the bodymind's internal symphony. She used the ancient Solveggio Tones, known for physical and spiritual reconnecting through the chakras, to create the soundtrack for *Sing and Hum Bumblebee*.

THE END